Someone Says

By

Carole

Lexa

Schaefer

Illustrated

by

Pierr

Morgan

VIKING

In the morning,
as always,
we line up
to go into school.

Someone says,
"Let's leapfrog in." And . . .

spring-boink, spring-sproink

we do.

Our teacher says,
"Time to sing our songs."

Someone says, "Let's make new ones."
And . . .

mi-fah-fah,

la-dee-dah

we do.

"Now," says our teacher.
"Everyone will draw Mei Lin."

Someone says, "Mei Lin can't stand still.
Let's draw her dancing like a pony."
And . . .

scribba-dibba,

clip-clop

we do.

We take out the blocks—
not enough for each of us to build a house.

Someone says,
"Let's make one tall house together."
And . . .

click-clack,

In the play yard,
the sun casts shivery shadows.

Someone says,
"Let's warm them up with our bird wings."
And . . .

floosh,

flash,

flip-flap

we do.

We jostle for our lunch boxes.
Someone says, "Grrr.

Let's eat up our noodles like tigers."
And . . .

slip,   sloop,

slurp

we do.

We walk home from school.
Someone says, "Yay!

What a great day! Let's dream up another."
And . . .

hush,   shush-a-bye

that is just what we do.

To the spirit, vision, and dreams of the child in each and every one of us, all over the world.

—Carole and Pierr

VIKING

Published by Penguin Group

Penguin Young Readers Group, 345 Hudson Street, New York, New York 10014, U.S.A.

Penguin Books Ltd, 80 Strand, London WC2R 0RL, England

Penguin Books Australia Ltd, 250 Camberwell Road, Camberwell, Victoria 3124, Australia

Penguin Books Canada Ltd, 10 Alcorn Avenue, Toronto, Ontario, Canada M4V 3B2

Penguin Books (N.Z.) Ltd, 182–190 Wairau Road, Auckland 10, New Zealand

First published in 2003 by Viking, a division of Penguin Young Readers Group

1 3 5 7 9 10 8 6 4 2

Text copyright © Carole Lexa Schaefer, 2003

Illustrations copyright © Pierr Morgan, 2003

All rights reserved

LIBRARY OF CONGRESS CATALOGING-IN-PUBLICATION DATA

Schaefer, Carole Lexa.

Someone says / by Carole Lexa Schaefer ; illustrated by Pierr Morgan.

p. cm.

Summary: A day at preschool has leaping frogs, dancing ponies, flapping wings, eating like tigers, and all the things that children can dream.

ISBN 0-670-03664-1

[1. Nursery schools–Fiction. 2. Schools–Fiction. 3. Imagination–Fiction. 4. Day–Fiction. 5. Bedtime–Fiction.] I. Morgan, Pierr, ill. II. Title.

PZ7.S3315Snt 2003   [E]–dc21   2003000952

Set in Tonic

Manufactured in China

Book design by Nancy Brennan